I am a little whale

François Crozat

I am a little whale. I was born in the warm waters of the Caribbean Sea.

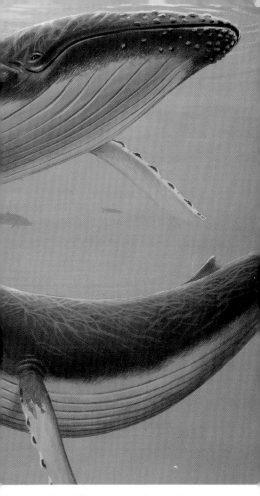

I grew inside my mother for ten months. Then I popped out.

My mother and her friend pushed me up to the surface to breathe.

Whales are not fish, so we can't breathe underwater.

Whenever I am hungry, my mother feeds me with her milk.

It is rich and delicious. I drink a lot of it, so I am growing very fast.

Now that I am big, I can explore this seaweed forest by myself.

Beautiful fish, pink and red coral, and other sea creatures live here.

When I see dangerous sharks or killer whales, I swim to Mom.

They don't dare to attack when she is there!

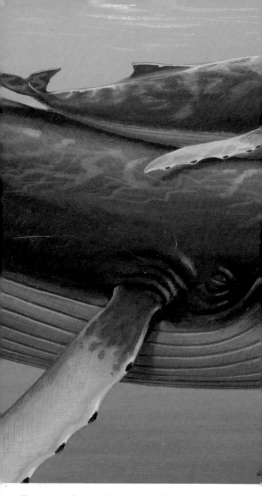

I am only a few months old, but I am bigger than you are.

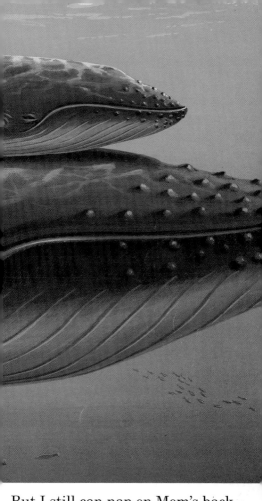

But I still can nap on Mom's back.
Here I sleep safe and sound.

Summer is coming. It is time for us to swim north.

A group of us swim thousands of
miles to a place called Greenland.

Here, huge icebergs float in the
water. Noisy sea gulls fly overhead.

And underneath the water there are millions of tiny shrimp.

Did you know we don't have teeth? Instead we have a kind of strainer.

It holds back the shrimp and tiny fish while we spit out the sea water.

After diving, I come to the surface
and blow out a shower of water.

Then I take in a deep breath and
I'm ready to dive for more food.

Whales are never too big to play!
Jumping is my favorite game.

I leap as high as I can, then I fall
back with a huge splash.

A boat sails by, but I am not afraid.
People don't hunt us anymore.